PELICAN

by Brian Wildsmith

PANTHEON BOOKS NEW YORK

Paul lived on a farm not far from the sea.

One day he went out for a walk along a country road. At last he came to his favorite tree. When he had climbed to the top, he looked down. He saw a truck, full of all kinds of things, coming down the road.

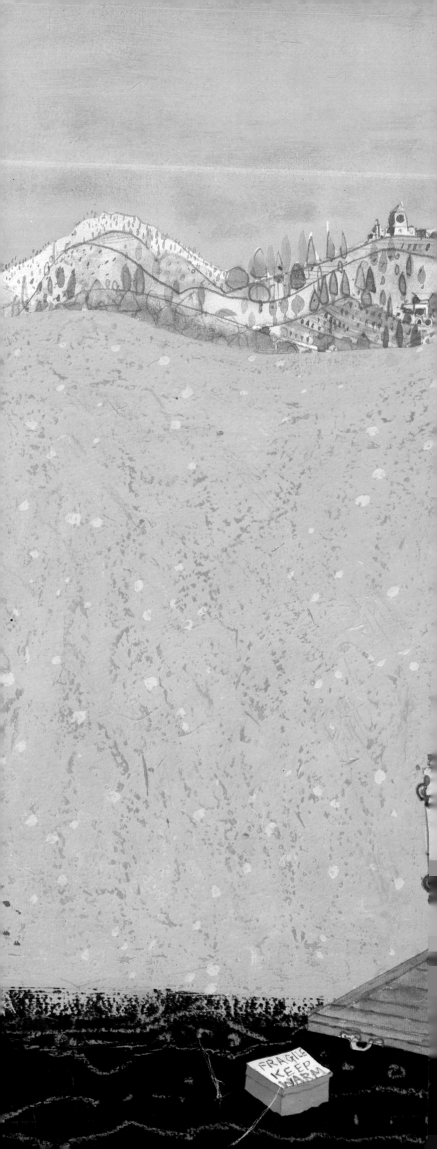

FRAGILE
KEEP
WARM

As the truck passed, it bounced
over a bump in the road, and a
small box fell off.

Paul climbed down the tree and
picked up the box carefully.
   He walked home and showed
it to his father.

Inside the box was a rather
large egg.

"What sort of an egg is this?"
he asked his father.

"I'm not sure," said his father.
"Take it to the speckled hen.
She'll hatch it, along with her
own eggs."

The speckled hen wasn't very pleased. But it was an egg, so she sat on it.

After a while all her other eggs hatched.

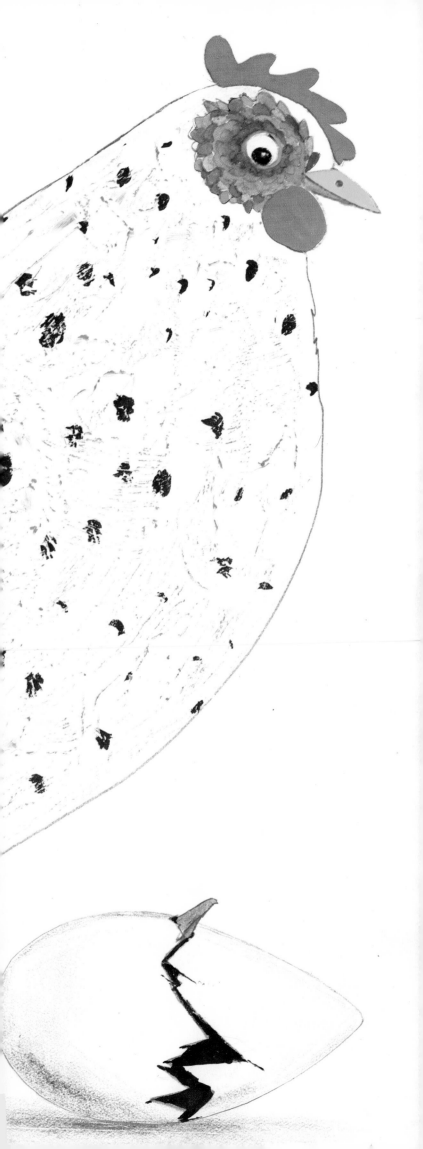

At last the large egg cracked,
and out came a strange-looking
bird.

"What sort of bird is this?"
asked everyone on the farm.

All the other chicks ate up their corn and soon grew big and strong.

The little bird only pecked at his food and didn't grow much at all.

The speckled hen tried to make him eat. But the little bird didn't seem to like the food.

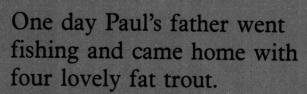

One day Paul's father went fishing and came home with four lovely fat trout.

"They'll make a grand meal for us tonight," said his wife. "I'll just go outside and feed the chicks, then I'll cook the fish."

The kitchen window was open. The little bird looked through and saw the fish.

He jumped inside and gobbled them up.

And every time the farmer brought home some fish, the little bird found them and ate them up. Soon he grew quite big.

"I know why he likes fish," Paul's mother said. "He must be a pelican. Look at his beak."

"Then let him catch his own fish!" shouted the farmer.

So Paul took the pelican to the river to catch fish. But the pelican didn't know what to do.

Then one day Paul took him to the port to see the fishing boats. "The fishermen can catch fish," said Paul. "Why can't you?"

And the pelican filled his beak with all their fish.

The fishermen were very angry. So was Paul's father, because he had to pay for all the fish the pelican ate.

"Why can't you teach him how to fish?" Paul's father yelled.

"He thought he was fishing," said Paul.

The next day Paul took the
pelican to a supermarket.

When the pelican saw the fish
counter, he tried to get at the fish
and knocked everything down.

Paul's father had to pay for
the damage. "I'm taking that
bird to the zoo tomorrow,"
he said.

That night when everyone was asleep, Paul climbed out of bed and got dressed.

He crept out of the house with the pelican. "I won't let them take you to the zoo," he said. "I'm going to take you to the land of the pelicans. There you'll learn how to catch fish."

They went to the port and
stowed away in a lifeboat on a
big ship.
   There they went to sleep.

In the morning the captain discovered them and woke them up.

"Have we reached the land of the pelicans?" asked Paul.

"No, we haven't even left port yet," said the captain. "What are you doing on my ship?"

So Paul told him.

The captain took them both to his car and drove them back home.

Paul's father and mother had been very worried and were relieved to see that Paul was all right.

"Listen," said his father. "If that bird means so much to you, then he can stay on the farm. But you'll have to teach him how to fish. And he'll have to help on the farm, like everybody else."

So in the evenings, Paul tried
to teach him to fish down by the
river.

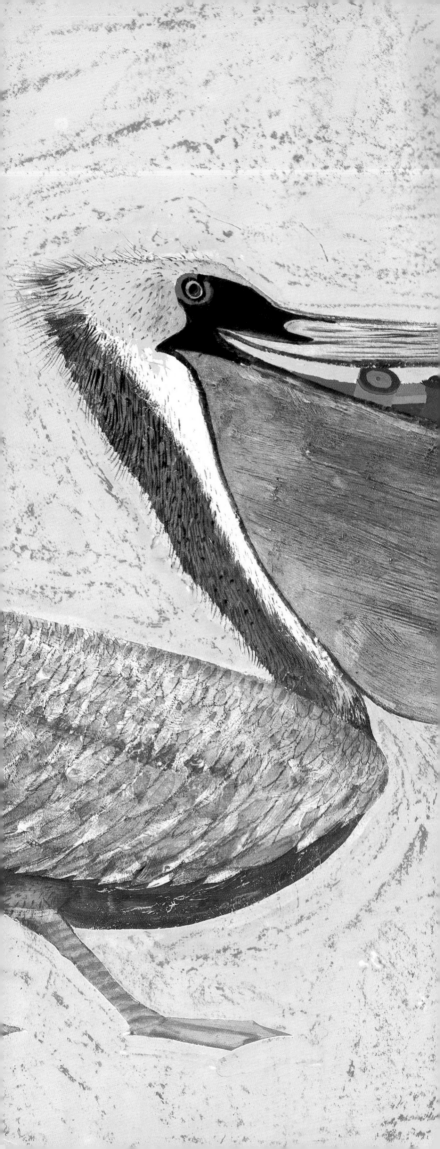

And during the day, the pelican was given jobs to do...like carrying groceries.

When Paul's father was working in the fields, the pelican carried his lunch out to him.

Paul's father grew quite fond of
the pelican, and sometimes gave
him a fish to eat.

One evening, Paul and the
pelican watched a kingfisher
dive into the water and catch
a fish.

"There! That's how you do
it," said Paul.

The pelican's eyes gleamed. He
flew into the air, dived into the
water, and caught his supper for
the very first time.

So from that time on, they
both went to the river every
evening, and the pelican caught
as much fish as he could eat.

The pelican grew bigger and
bigger.

One evening by the water's
edge, he came up to Paul and
stroked him gently with his
wings. Then he flew into the air,
dived into the river, and caught
a fish. He circled high over Paul
and flew away out of sight.

Paul waited for him. But he did
not come back. Slowly Paul
walked home.

   "Don't be sad," said Paul's
father. "He's got to be with other
pelicans now. That's where he
will be really happy."

The bird flew away to the land
of the pelicans.

But there was something that
neither Paul nor his father had
ever known about the pelican.

But the pelican had known all the time.

And in the land of the pelicans she lived happily ever after.

The beginning.

Library of Congress Cataloging in Publication Data
Wildsmith, Brian. Pelican.
Summary: When a pelican hatches from the large egg Paul finds,
he must teach the bird how to fish.
[1. Pelicans—Fiction]   I. Title.
PZ7.W647 Pe   1983   [E]   82-12431
ISBN 0-394-85668-6
ISBN 0-394-95668-0 (lib. bdg.)